MIGHTY ROBOT

vs. THE MUTANT MOSQUITOES FROM MERCURY

STORY BY
DAV PILKEY

ART BY
DAN SANTAT

SCHOLASTIC

FOR A.J., KATIE, JOSH, BECKY, AND ADAM BUTLER
– D.P.

FOR JODI
– D.S.

Scholastic Children's Books
An imprint of Scholastic Ltd
Euston House, 24 Eversholt Street
London, NW1 1DB, UK
Registered office: Westfield Road, Southam, Warwickshire, CV47 0RA
SCHOLASTIC and associated logos are trademarks and/or registered
trademarks of Scholastic Inc.

First published in the US by Scholastic Inc, 2000
First published in the UK by Scholastic Ltd, 2001
This edition published 2014

Text copyright © Dav Pilkey, 2000, 2014
Illustrations copyright © Dan Santat, 2014

The rights of Dav Pilkey and Dan Santat to be identified as the author and illustrator of this
work have been asserted by them.

ISBN 978 1407 14334 7

A CIP catalogue record for this book is available from the British Library.

Printed in Italy
Papers used by Scholastic Children's Books are made from wood grown in
sustainable forests.

1 3 5 7 9 10 8 6 4 2

www.scholastic.co.uk

CHAPTERS

CHAPTER ONE
RICKY AND HIS ROBOT

There once was a mouse named
Ricky Ricotta who lived in
Squeakyville with his mother
and father.

Ricky Ricotta might have been
the smallest mouse around . . .

. . . but he had the BIGGEST
best friend in town.

CHAPTER TWO
SCHOOL DAYS

Ricky and his Mighty Robot
liked to go to school together.

Sometimes when Ricky was running late, his Robot would fly him straight to the front door.

After school, the Mighty Robot liked to help Ricky with his homework. The Robot's computer brain could solve complex maths problems . . .

. . . his finger had a built-in pencil sharpener . . .

. . . and he could even remove his telescopic eyeball, which made studying the planets much easier.

"Wow," said Ricky. "I can see all the way to Mercury! That's cool!"

CHAPTER THREE
MR MOSQUITO
HATES MERCURY!

Mercury was the smallest planet in the solar system, and it was the closest planet to the sun. But it certainly was not *cool*!

Just ask Mr Mosquito.
He lived on Mercury, and he
HATED everything about it!

He hated the long, *long*, HOT days. Each day on Mercury, the temperature rose to more than eight hundred degrees!

Mr Mosquito couldn't even walk down the street because his flip-flops always melted on the pavement.

Mr Mosquito hated Mercury's long, *long*, COLD nights, too. Each night on Mercury, the temperature dropped to almost three hundred degrees below zero!

Mr Mosquito couldn't even brush his teeth because his toothpaste was always frozen solid!

"I've g-g-got to g-g-get away f-f-from th-th-this awful p-p-planet," said Mr Mosquito, shivering in the cold. So Mr Mosquito looked at his view screen and saw the planet Earth.

He saw mice playing happily on cool autumn days.

He saw them sleeping soundly on warm summer nights.

"Earth is the planet for me!" said Mr Mosquito. "Soon it will be mine!"

CHAPTER FOUR
MR MOSQUITO MAKES HIS MOVE

Mr Mosquito went into his secret laboratory and clipped his filthy fingernails.

He put the clippings into a giant machine and zapped them with a powerful ray.

Then Mr Mosquito's fingernails
grew and grew and grew . . .

. . . into massive Mutant Mosquitoes!
Mr Mosquito climbed aboard his
spaceship and called to his troops.

"Mutant Mosquitoes," he cried,
"it is time to conquer Earth!
Follow me!"

And they did.

CHAPTER FIVE
THE MOSQUITOES ATTACK

When Mr Mosquito got to Earth,
he ordered his Mutant Mosquitoes
to attack Squeakyville.

Ricky was in his maths class that afternoon. He looked out of the window and saw the Mutant Mosquitoes.

"Uh-oh," said Ricky. "It looks like Squeakyville needs our help!"

Ricky raised his hand.

"May I be excused?" Ricky asked his teacher. "My Robot and I have to save the Earth."

"Not until you've finished your maths test," said Ricky's teacher.

Ricky had three problems left. "What is two times three?" he asked himself aloud.

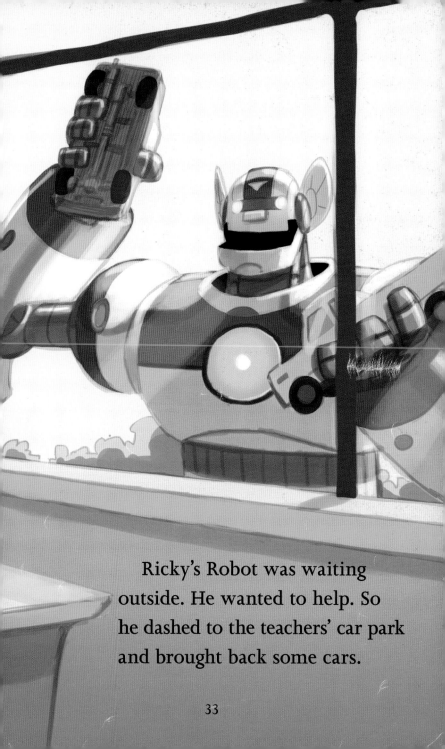

Ricky's Robot was waiting
outside. He wanted to help. So
he dashed to the teachers' car park
and brought back some cars.

Ricky's Robot put three cars into one pile, and he put three cars into another pile.

Ricky looked at the piles of cars.
"*Two* piles of *three* cars," said
Ricky. "Two times three equals *six*!"

Ricky looked at his next question.
"What is *six* minus *five*?" he asked.
Ricky's Robot knew just what to do.

He threw five of the cars back
into the car park.

"I get it," said Ricky. "Six minus
five equals *one*!"

Ricky's last question was the hardest of all. "What is *one* divided by *two*?" he asked.

The Robot used his mighty karate chop to divide one car in two.

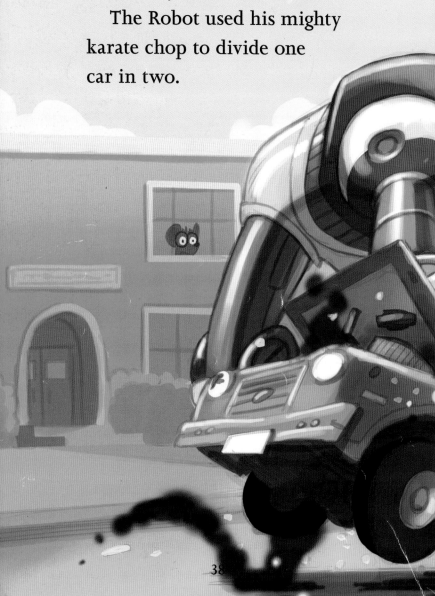

"That was easy," said Ricky. "One divided by two equals *one-half*!"

Ricky handed in his test. Then he climbed out of the window.

"Let's go, Mighty Robot," said Ricky. "We've got to save the Earth."

"M-M-M-My *car!*" cried Ricky's teacher.

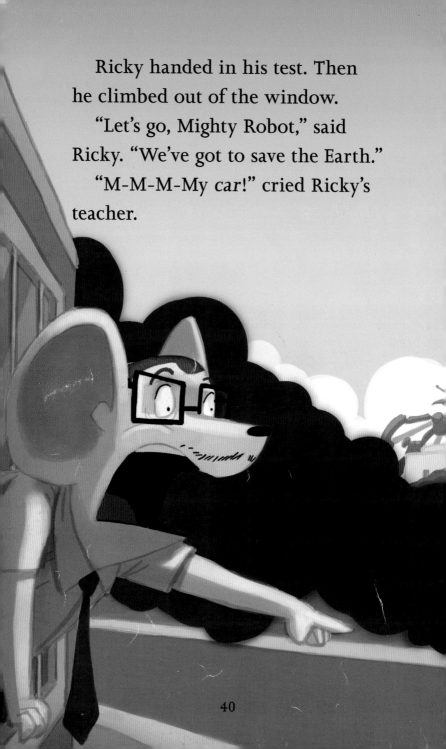

CHAPTER SIX
THE HEROES ARRIVE

Ricky and his Mighty Robot ran downtown to face the Mutant Mosquitoes.

The Mosquitoes attacked
Ricky's Robot.

"Hey," said Ricky. "Four against
one is not fair!"

Then Ricky had an idea. "Come with me, Robot," said Ricky.

The Mighty Robot was busy fighting, so he could not follow Ricky. But his arm could stretch very far!

Ricky and his Robot's arm stretched all the way to the Bugs Away bug-spray factory.

Ricky told the Robot's arm to grab one of the huge bug-spray storage tanks.

Then they headed back to the battle.

CHAPTER SEVEN
A BUGGY BATTLE

The Robot shook the tank of bug spray.

The Robot sprayed the Mosquitoes.

Then he broke up the buggy battle
with a big blast from his bionic boot!

CHAPTER EIGHT
MR MOSQUITO'S REVENGE

The Mutant Mosquitoes had been defeated. Ricky's Mighty Robot chased them into space.

The Mosquitoes flew back to Mercury and never bothered anybody again.

Mr Mosquito was very angry.
He grabbed Ricky and took him
into his spaceship. "Help me, Robot!"
Ricky cried.

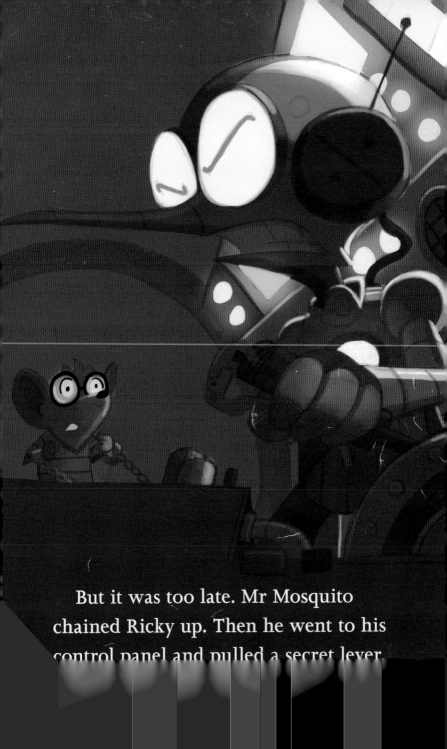

But it was too late. Mr Mosquito chained Ricky up. Then he went to his control panel and pulled a secret lever.

Suddenly, his spaceship began
to change. It shifted . . .

. . . and grew . . .

. . . and transformed into a giant
Mecha-Mosquito!

The Mecha-Mosquito attacked Ricky's Mighty Robot. But Ricky's Robot would not fight back.

He knew that Ricky was inside the
Mecha-Mosquito, and he did not want
his best friend to get hurt.

The Mecha-Mosquito pounded
Ricky's Robot.

What could Ricky do?

Ricky thought and thought. Then he had an idea.

"Mr Mosquito," said Ricky, "I have to go to the bathroom."

"Not now," said Mr Mosquito. "I am too busy beating up your Robot!"

"But it's an emergency," said Ricky.

"All right, all right," said Mr Mosquito.
He unlocked Ricky's chains and led him
to the boys' toilets.

"Hurry up in there!" he yelled.

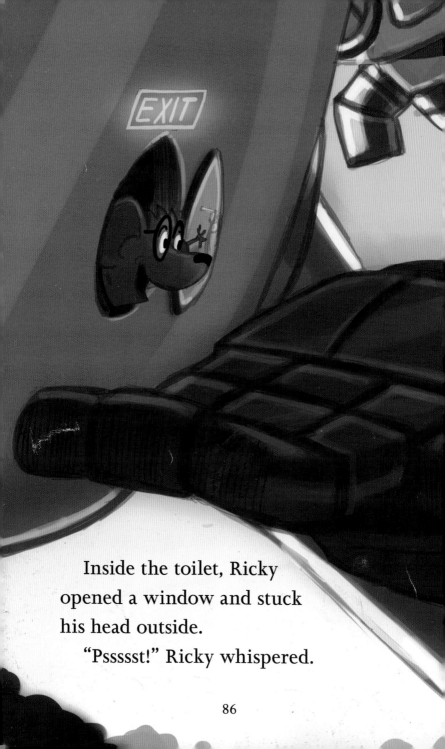

Inside the toilet, Ricky opened a window and stuck his head outside.

"Pssssst!" Ricky whispered.

The Robot saw Ricky, and he held out his giant hand.

Ricky jumped.

"I'm safe," said Ricky. "Now it will be a fair fight!"

CHAPTER NINE
RICKY'S ROBOT STRIKES BACK

Inside the Mecha-Mosquito, Mr Mosquito was getting very angry. He knocked on the toilet door. "Let's hurry up in there!" he yelled. "I haven't got all da—"

KER-POW!
Ricky's Robot punched the
Mecha-Mosquito right in the face.

Mr Mosquito leaped to his control panel and fought back hard. The final battle was about to begin.

CHAPTER TEN
THE FINAL BATTLE
(IN FLIP-O-RAMA™)

-RAMA
HERE'S HOW IT WORKS!

STEP 1

Place your *left* hand inside the dotted lines marked "LEFT HAND HERE". Hold the book open *flat*.

STEP 2

Grasp the *right-hand* page with your right thumb and index finger (inside the dotted lines marked "RIGHT THUMB HERE").

STEP 3

Now *quickly* flip the right-hand page back and forth until the picture appears to be *animated*.

(For extra fun, try adding your own sound-effects!)

FLIP-O-RAMA 1
(pages 97 and 99)

Remember, flip *only* page 97.
While you are flipping, be sure you
can see the picture on page 97
and the one on page 99.
If you flip quickly, the two
pictures will start to look like
<u>one</u> *animated* picture.

Don't forget to add
your own sound-effects!

LEFT HAND HERE

THE MECHA-MOSQUITO
ATTACKED.

97

RIGHT
THUMB
HERE

THE MECHA-MOSQUITO ATTACKED.

FLIP-O-RAMA 2
(pages 101 and 103)

Remember, flip *only* page 101.
While you are flipping, be sure you
can see the picture on page 101
and the one on page 103.
If you flip quickly, the two
pictures will start to look like
<u>one</u> *animated* picture.

Don't forget to add
your own sound-effects!

LEFT HAND HERE

**RICKY'S ROBOT
FOUGHT BACK.**

RIGHT
THUMB
HERE

RICKY'S ROBOT
FOUGHT BACK.

FLIP-O-RAMA 3

(pages 105 and 107)

Remember, flip *only* page 105.
While you are flipping, be sure you
can see the picture on page 105
and the one on page 107.
If you flip quickly, the two
pictures will start to look like
<u>one</u> *animated* picture.

Don't forget to add
your own sound-effects!

LEFT HAND HERE

THE MECHA-MOSQUITO
BATTLED HARD.

RIGHT
THUMB
HERE

THE MECHA-MOSQUITO
BATTLED HARD.

FLIP-O-RAMA 4

(pages 109 and 111)

Remember, flip *only* page 109.
While you are flipping, be sure you
can see the picture on page 109
and the one on page 111.
If you flip quickly, the two
pictures will start to look like
<u>one</u> *animated* picture.

Don't forget to add
your own sound-effects!

LEFT HAND HERE

RICKY'S ROBOT
BATTLED HARDER.

RIGHT
THUMB
HERE

RICKY'S ROBOT
BATTLED HARDER.

FLIP-O-RAMA 5

(pages 113 and 115)

Remember, flip *only* page 113.
While you are flipping, be sure you
can see the picture on page 113
and the one on page 115.
If you flip quickly, the two
pictures will start to look like
<u>one</u> *animated* picture.

Don't forget to add
your own sound-effects!

LEFT HAND HERE

RICKY'S ROBOT
SAVED THE DAY!

RIGHT
THUMB
HERE

RICKY'S ROBOT
SAVED THE DAY!

CHAPTER ELEVEN
JUSTICE PREVAILS

The Mecha-Mosquito had been destroyed, and Ricky Ricotta's Mighty Robot was victorious.

Mr Mosquito crawled out of his damaged ship and began to cry. "What a bad day I am having!" cried Mr Mosquito.

"It's about to get worse," said Ricky.

Ricky's Mighty Robot picked up
Mr Mosquito and dropped him into
the Squeakyville prison.

Then Ricky and his Mighty Robot
flew home for chocolate milk and
grilled cheese sandwiches.

"You boys have saved the world again," said Ricky's mother.

"Yes," said Ricky's father. "Thank you for sticking together and fighting for what was right!"

"No problem," said Ricky . . .

. . . "that's what friends are for."

RICKY RICOTTA
AND HIS MIGHTY ROBOT
ARE BEST BUDDIES – BUT WITH BIG
FRIENDS COME BIG RESPONSIBILITIES. . . .

Find out what happens when Ricky's parents decide to teach the boys a lesson about being responsible in their next adventure, *Ricky Ricotta's Mighty Robot vs. the Voodoo Vultures from Venus!*

READY FOR

MORE RICKY?

DAV PILKEY

has written and illustrated more than fifty books for children, including *The Paperboy*, a Caldecott Honor book; *Dog Breath: The Horrible Trouble with Hally Tosis*, winner of the California Young Reader Medal; and the IRA Children's Choice *Dumb Bunnies* series. He is also the creator of the *New York Times* best-selling *Captain Underpants* books. Dav lives in the Pacific Northwest with his wife. Find him online at www.pilkey.com.

DAN SANTAT

is the writer and illustrator of the picture book *The Adventures of Beekle: The Unimaginary Friend*. He is also the creator of the graphic novel *Sidekicks* and has illustrated many acclaimed picture books, including the *New York Times* bestseller *Because I'm Your Dad* by Ahmet Zappa and *Crankenstein* by Samantha Berger. Dan also created the Disney animated hit *The Replacements*. He lives in Southern California with his family. Find him online at www.dantat.com.